I0749449

Chloe Annabel – Chloe.Shipp@hotmail.com

ISBN: 978-0-9955922-4-7
Published by Annabel Arts, 2025

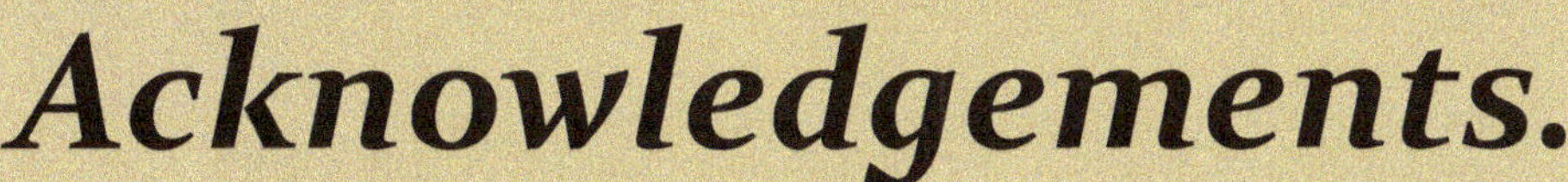

Acknowledgements.

To my daughters,
Arwen Lily and Artemis Rose
this is for you.

I'm a pair of shoes I was born in France, the beautiful country, in its capital, Paris.

Made of pure leather, the finest money can buy, I remember the day I came to life, like it was yesterday. A skilled man cut me from a long sheet of leather and carefully shaped me to size. He stretched me over a model of the shoe I would become. He snipped, glued, and smoothed until I was perfect.

Then, I was placed in a dark space, so dark I couldn't see a thing. The next time I opened my eyes, I was staring out of a huge transparent sheet of glass; or at least, I think that's what humans called it.

Sometime later, a young, beautiful woman came. Picked me up and took me away. For the next few days, I rested in a soft, cozy closet, surrounded by other elegant shoes like myself. Then one day, she returned and slipped me onto her feet.

We went to a grand event—bright lights, flashing cameras, and a long, beautiful red carpet. People shouted her name as we walked. It was an incredible experience, one I will never forget.

But after that magical night, she didn't return me to the closet. Instead, she tossed me into a plastic bag. I didn't understand, hadn't she loved me? I was beautiful! She had only worn me once!

The bag moved and shifted for what felt like forever, bumping side to side. Where was I going? I felt forgotten. Worthless. Then one day, the bag opened, and I saw a brilliant white light shining down on me.

Had I died and gone to the big shoe store in the sky?

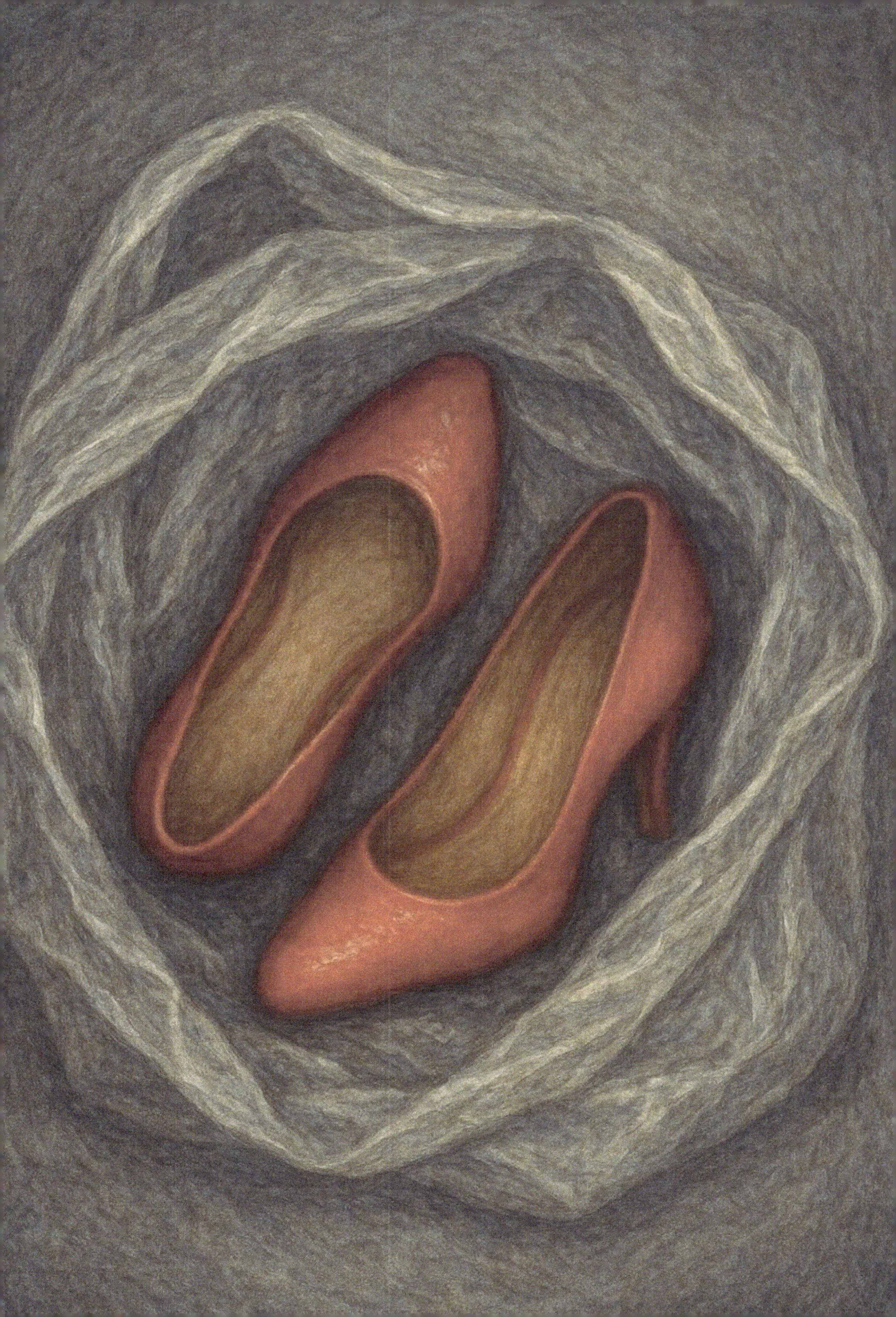

No. I was in a new shop. But not like before - this one was full of old, worn-out, and discarded shoes.

I sat on a dusty shelf, waiting, hoping.

Then one day, a young girl came. She looked up at me, then smiled. I was then taken down from the shelf and whisked away to another home.

There, I was put into a small box, not a dark one this time, but a box full of clothes and different, odd little treasures.

A few days later, she came back, took me out and slipped me on. She dressed in her other colourful, quirky clothes and paraded around. She tripped a few times - I was far too big for her little feet - but she didn’t mind. She giggled.

She placed me back into the box, but from time to time she returned. Each time, she would try me on, walk around clumsily, and before putting me away, she'd stroke my leathery skin and whisper to me how much she loved me.

Now I know I have found a loving home. It may not be one of the most comfortable of places, or the most luxurious, but I just needed to be wanted, and this is where I remain to this day.

Now, my little girl has grown into a vibrant, elegant, young woman. She wears me all the time - to parties, on walks—you name it, I'm there.

I'm no longer just a pair of shoes. I'm a part of her story. And I'll be here, by her side, for as long as she'll have me.

THE
END

TIME FOR SOME FUN!

Can you spot the
different pairs
Scarlet Shoes in the
following pictures?

ANTIQUE
Scarlet Shoes

CAFE

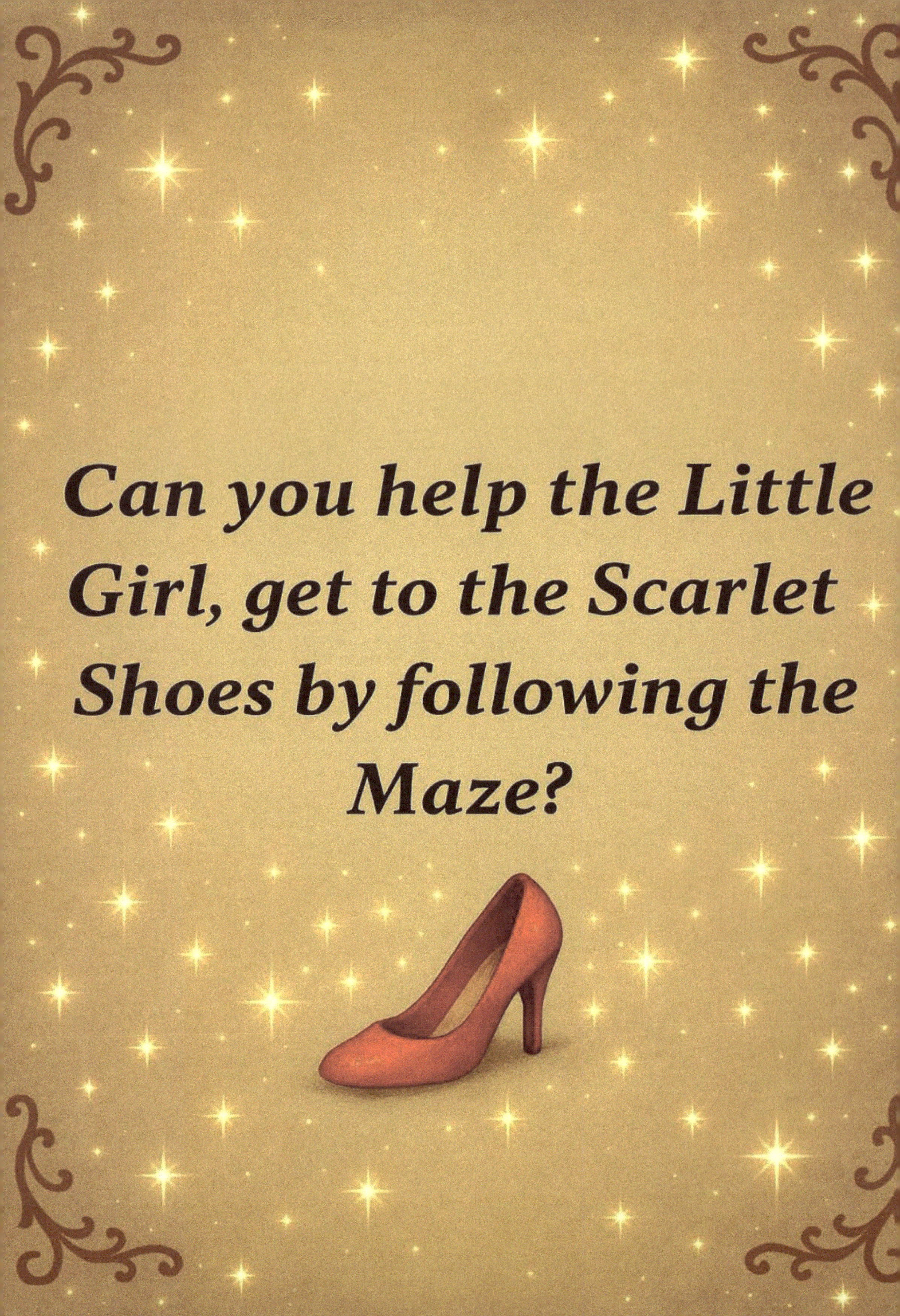
Can you help the Little Girl, get to the Scarlet Shoes by following the Maze?

Spot the Difference, Look Closely!

BOUTIQUE
Chausse
CHAUSSIRE

SHOES

SHOES

www.ingramcontent.com/pod-product-compliance
Lightning Source LLC
Chambersburg PA
CBHW041538010726
47507CB00010B/400

* 9 7 8 0 9 9 5 5 9 2 2 4 7 *